ZOO-LOOKING

ZOO-LOOKING

Mem Fox

illustrated by
Candace Whitman

MONDO

The illustrations were done in collage. The papers were painted with watercolor
and then torn into the shapes used to make each picture.

This edition first published in the United States of America in 1996 by
MONDO Publishing

By arrangement with MULTIMEDIA INTERNATIONAL (UK) LTD

For information contact:
MONDO Publishing
980 Avenue of the Americas
New York, New York 10018
Visit our web site at http://www.mondopub.com

Printed in Hong Kong by South China Printing Co. (1988) Ltd.
First MONDO printing, February 1996

02 03 04 05 06 07   9 8

Text originally published in Australia in 1986 by Horwitz Publications Pty Ltd
Original development by Robert Anderson & Associates and Snowball Educational
Designed by Kimberly M. Adlerman
Production by Danny Adlerman

Library of Congress Cataloging-in-Publication Data
Fox, Mem, 1946-
    Zoo-looking / Mem Fox ; illustrated by Candace Whitman.
        p.   cm.
    Summary: While Flora visits the zoo with her father, not only does she look at
the animals but some of them turn to look at her.
    ISBN 1-57255-010-4 (reinforced hc : alk. paper). — ISBN 1-57255-011-2
(pbk. : alk. paper). — ISBN 1-57255-012-0 (big book)
    [1. Zoo animals—Fiction. 2. Zoos—Fiction. 3. Fathers and daughters—Fiction.
4. Hispanic Americans—Fiction. 5. Stories in rhyme.] I. Whitman, Candace, 1958-
ill. II. Title.
PZ8.3.F8245Zo   1996
[E]—dc20
                                                            95-14171
                                                            CIP
                                                            AC

One day Flora went to the zoo.

She looked at the giraffe
and the giraffe looked back.

She looked at the panther
with its coat of silky black.

She looked at the tiger
and the tiger looked back.

She looked at the snake
as it slithered through a crack.

She looked at the penguin
and the penguin looked back.

She looked at the monkey
as its baby got a smack.

She looked at the ostrich
and the ostrich looked back.

She looked at the zebra
whose tail went *whack!*

She looked at the koala
and the koala looked back.

She looked at the bear
as it gobbled up a snack.

She looked at the gorilla
and the gorilla looked back.

She looked at the camel
with the humps upon its back.

She looked at the elephant
next to the yak.

She looked at her dad
and he *smiled* back.